Way to Go, Zoe!

By Kara McMahon

Illustrated by Tom Brannon

 Dalmatian Press, LLC, 2009. All rights reserved.
Published by Dalmatian Press, LLC, 2009. The DALMATIAN PRESS name and logo are trademarks of Dalmatian Press, LLC, Franklin, Tennessee 37067. No part of this book may be reproduced or copied in any form without written permission from the copyright owner.

Printed in the U.S.A.
ISBN: 1-40375-321-0

08 09 10 11 BM 10 9 8 7 6 5 4 3 2 1
17654 Sesame Street 8x8 Storybook: Way to Go, Zoe!

*H*onk! Honk!

It was early morning on Sesame Street. No geese were flying in the sky. The Honkers were still asleep. So who was honking?

Honk! Honk!

Only one other thing on Sesame Street honked like that—the horn on the Zoe-mobile!

Honk! Honk!
"Good morning!" Zoe called out from the Zoe-mobile. "Rise and shine!"
Honk!
"Gee, Zoe," said Baby Bear. "Isn't it a little early to be honking that horn? You're going to wake up everybody on Sesame Street."

"Sorry—maybe it *is* a little early," said Zoe. "I guess I love honking and driving so much that sometimes I forget that not everyone wants to hear my horn!"

I Love Noise!

Honk! Honk! Zoe drove on down Sesame Street. She tried to be quiet, but she couldn't resist a honk here and there.

Before long, Zoe woke up the whole neighborhood!

Everyone wanted to honk the horn—first Elmo . . .

and then Rosita . . .

Bert was next . . .

I wonder if I can use the
horn to call pigeons?

Zoe *tried* to wait patiently for everyone
to have a turn—she really
did—but finally . . .

"My turn!" cried Zoe. "Are you ready to hear a really *amazing, super-duper honk?*"

She raised the horn over her head, squeezed the honker as hard as she could, and . . . *nothing happened!* The horn didn't make a sound— not even a teeny squeak, much less a big, loud honk!

"Try it again, Zoe," Elmo said.

So Zoe squeezed it again . . . and *again* nothing happened!

"Oh no!" she wailed. "My horn is broken! I can't drive the Zoe-mobile without my horn! What am I going to do?"

"Elmo knows!" Elmo told Zoe. "Zoe can ask Luis and Maria to fix the horn! They always help Elmo when one of Elmo's toys gets broken."

"But Luis and Maria are on vacation until tomorrow," Zoe replied. "I can't wait until tomorrow. I want to drive the Zoe-mobile today!"

"Could you fix the horn yourself, Zoe?" Rosita asked.
"I don't know *how* to fix a horn!" Zoe replied, shaking her head.

"Maybe you could use something else instead of a horn," Bert suggested.

Zoe looked doubtful.

"Zoe could try using Elmo's giggle," Elmo offered.

"Well, okay, Elmo," she finally said. "Try running next to me as I drive."

"Elmo . . . can't . . . run . . . that . . . fast . . ." Elmo panted as he tried to keep up with Zoe. "And Elmo . . . cannot . . . giggle . . . and run!"

"Well, that didn't work," Zoe said when she stopped. "But thanks for trying, Elmo."

"What else could I use for a horn?" Zoe asked.

"Hey, Ernie," Bert whispered. "Are you thinking what I'm thinking?"

"I wasn't thinking anything, Bert, old buddy!" Ernie replied.

"Oh, Ernie—think!" Bert groaned. "You have something that makes a noise when you squeeze it—something that Zoe could use for a horn!"

Bert pointed to Ernie's Rubber Duckie.
"Gee, I don't know, Bert," Ernie said slowly.
But before Ernie could make up his mind, Bert said,
"Hey, Zoe—we have an idea!"

Zoe took Rubber Duckie and gave him a squeeze. *Squeak! Squeak!*
"That works perfectly!" Bert exclaimed.
"Thanks a lot, you guys," Zoe said happily.
"Don't squeeze too hard, Zoe!" Ernie called as she drove away.

Zoe thought about how much she loved her horn,
and how hard it had been for her to share it with her friends. She had
a feeling that Ernie wouldn't really want to share his favorite toy for
the whole day.

So Zoe gave Rubber Duckie back to him. "Thanks for letting me try,
Ernie," she said. "But a squeak just isn't the same as a honk."

Then Zoe thought about Rosita's suggestion. "Maybe I *could* fix the horn myself. But I wonder where I should start."

So Zoe looked at the horn and scratched her head. "I know that I have to squeeze the soft part to make the honking noise," she said. She squeezed. Nothing happened. But *why* didn't it make a sound? she wondered.

Zoe peered closely at the black rubber squeezer.

"Look!" she announced. "My horn is torn! That's why it's not honking! And I know *exactly* how to fix it!"

Zoe drove over to Hooper's Store. She quickly came back with a bandage, just like the kind she put on her knee when she had a scrape.

Rosita held the horn while Zoe carefully smoothed the bandage over the tear.

HONK! HONK! HONK!

"I fixed it!" Zoe yelled, giving her horn a big, happy squeeze.

"I knew you could do it!" Rosita told her.

"Well, *I* didn't know I could," Zoe said. "That is, until I gave it a try!"

HONK HONK!

"Way to go, Zoe!" her friends said proudly.

And away she went!